THE ARABIAN NIGHTS

CHILDREN'S COLLECTION

First published in the UK by Sweet Cherry Publishing Limited, 2023
Unit 36, Vulcan House, Vulcan Road,
Leicester, LE5 3EF, United Kingdom

Sweet Cherry Europe (Europe address)
Nauschgasse 4/3/2 POB 1017
Vienna, WI 1220, Austria

2 4 6 8 10 9 7 5 3 1

ISBN: 978-1-78226-841-3

The Arabian Nights Children's Collection:
The Magic Horse

© Sweet Cherry Publishing Limited, 2023

Text based on translations of the original folk tale,
adapted by Kellie Jones
Illustrations by Sarah Grace

All rights reserved. No part of this publication may be
reproduced or utilised in any form or by any means, electronic
or mechanical, including photocopying, recording, or using
any information storage and retrieval system, without prior
permission in writing from the publisher.

The right of Kellie Jones to be identified as the author of this work
has been asserted by them in accordance with the Copyright,
Designs and Patents Act 1988.

www.sweetcherrypublishing.com

Printed and bound in India

The Magic Horse

Sweet Cherry

Long ago, in the ancient lands of Arabia, there lived a brave woman called Scheherazade. When the country's sultan went mad, Scheherazade used her cleverness and creativity to save many lives – including her own. She did this over a thousand and one nights, by telling the sultan stories of adventure, danger and enchantment.

This is just one of them …

The King of Persia
He was gifted the magic horse

Prince Firouz
The King of Persia's son

The Sultan of Kashmir
The sultan and leader of the horsemen in Kashmir

Princess Ameera
The King of Bengal's daughter

The King of Bengal
Princess Ameera's father

Sathvik
He gifted the magic horse to the king

Aditi
A Kashmiri maid

Chapter 1

Of all the festivals to celebrate the New Year, the oldest and most splendid was held in Persia. There the day was spent playing games, watching spectacles and feasting on food and drink.

It was also a time when people showed their loyalty to the King of Persia. They did this by giving him beautiful and rare gifts in

> **Persia**
> *An ancient empire in southwestern Asia, now called Iran.*

return for his royal favour.

One year, just as the festivities were drawing to a close, three men came before the king and his son with three most unusual gifts. The first was a golden peacock that would flap its wings and squawk at the end of each hour. The king, who was a collector of strange and wonderful inventions, was delighted.

'What can I give you in exchange for this gift?' he asked.

'Sire,' replied the first man, 'I have heard much of your two

royal favour
To have a royal person's favour is to have their approval, liking or good will.

beautiful daughters. I would like your permission to marry the eldest.'

'First, I must make sure your gift works,' replied the king. So they waited for the hour to pass and for the bird to flap its wings and squawk as promised.

'Very well,' replied the king, 'if my daughter has no objection to you, you may marry her.' And the man was taken away to meet the eldest princess and see if she was willing.

The second man brought forward a brass trumpet that would play itself whenever a weapon was drawn in the king's presence, alerting him to danger.

The prince tested this with his own sword.

'What can I give you in exchange for this gift?' the king asked.

'Sire,' replied the second man, 'I too have heard much of your beautiful daughters. I would like your permission to marry your youngest.'

'Very well,' replied the king, 'if she has no objection, you may marry her.' And the man was taken away to meet the youngest princess and see if she was willing.

The third man who came forwards was scowling, because

there were no daughters left to marry. Behind him was an ebony horse that looked just like a real one. It had a wreath of flowers around its neck.

'Your Majesty,' he said, 'my name is Sathvik. I believe my gift will outshine all others.'

The king raised his eyebrows at this boast, and his son laughed.

'I see nothing but a toy,' said the prince. 'It has excellent craftsmanship indeed, but not more than any skilled carpenter might show.'

ebony
A hard black or dark brown wood.

Sathvik's scowl deepened. 'I do not speak of how it looks,' he said; 'I speak of what it can do.'

'And what can it do?' asked the king.

'Sire, you have only to sit upon this horse and think of a place you would like to go – no matter how far – and it will take you there.'

The king looked again at the offering. Truly it was a thing of beauty, with dark wood polished to an inky sheen, and the silken threads of its mane and tail finely braided with white beads. But take

craftsmanship
The skill of making and crafting things.

anyone anywhere? That he could not believe – and he said so.

'Perhaps His Royal Highness the prince would like to test it?' suggested Sathvik, sullenly.

Bristling at Sathvik's tone, and keen to prove that he was lying, the prince climbed onto the red velvet saddle. As he took the golden reins, Sathvik pointed to a peg in the right side of the horse's neck.

'You turn this peg clockwise to fly,' he said, 'and–'

But rather than wait for him to finish explaining, the prince had already turned the peg.

The moment he did, much to his surprise, the horse soared into the sky. The whole court erupted with excitement and the prince was soon lost from sight.

Everyone waited for his return. And waited. And waited …

They waited so long that everyone – especially Sathvik – grew nervous.

'Your Majesty,' he said to the king, 'you may recall that the prince did not wait for me to finish my instructions. If he had, I would have told him that he needs to turn the peg *anti*clockwise in order to land.'

The king was furious. 'Are you telling me that my son has no idea how to land that thing? He could be flying around forever?'

'It was not my fault, Sire! He may yet figure it out and turn the peg for himself.'

'And what is to stop him plummeting to his death if he figures it out over the desert or the middle of the ocean?'

'The horse will only land where the rider wills it to, Sire. The prince will be safe, I am sure of it.'

'Your assurance is not good enough,' said the king. 'Guards! Seize him. Till my son returns he is my prisoner.'

'No, Sire! Please!' Sathvik begged as he was dragged away to the dungeons, but the king's only response was to shout after him: 'Believe me, if my son does not return within a month, your fate will be far worse!'

assurance
A positive way of speaking to make someone else feel confident.

Chapter 2

The prince, whose name was Firouz, had not thought of a destination other than up when he mounted the magic horse. So that was where he went.

For a full hour he rose higher and higher into the sky, until he feared he would hit his head on the top if there was one. Below him trees and buildings, villages and cities fell away.

When he could no longer tell the mountains from the plains, he began to think about landing.

He reasoned that because there was a peg in the right side of the horse's neck that made it go up, there must be another peg in the left side that made it go down. Even in the growing darkness, he soon found that there was not. Not in the neck, not near the saddle, and not anywhere else he could reach or see.

'Down!' he commanded the horse. 'Descend!' But the horse continued to climb. 'Lower! Land!' No matter what word he used, none worked.

'Be calm,' Firouz told himself,

as panic began to set in. He tried to remember Sathvik's explanation. 'You turn this screw clockwise to fly and ...' *then what*? he thought.

Firouz returned his attention to the peg. It would not turn further forward, so instead he turned it back, anticlockwise to its original position. Immediately, the horse began to descend. The prince gave a sigh of relief.

It was past midnight by the time Firouz and the horse touched down – though midnight *where* he did not know. The complex carvings and domed rooftops of his homeland had been replaced with curving shadows and pyramid shapes. It was similar to home, but it felt different.

He was outside a marble palace. In one corner of the courtyard he found a door that led to a staircase. Only a prince would have dared to enter a foreign palace, but Firouz trusted that no one would harm him once they saw that he was unarmed.

Still, it was dark and he was in a strange place, so he went cautiously up the stairs. On a landing he noticed an open door, beyond which was a dimly lit hall. By the light of a lantern hanging from the ceiling, he saw two guards sleeping, each with a naked sword beside him.

unarmed
To be without a weapon.

He thought about letting them know he was there, but he would be no match for them if they woke startled and defensive. *What are they guarding, anyway?* he wondered. *Or whom?*

He left the guards snoring and crept on down the hall. At the far end he could see a curtain and a light beyond it. Inside he found a magnificent chamber full of women asleep on cushions on the floor, except for one who slept on a bed. *She must be the one they are guarding,* he decided. *A princess, perhaps?*

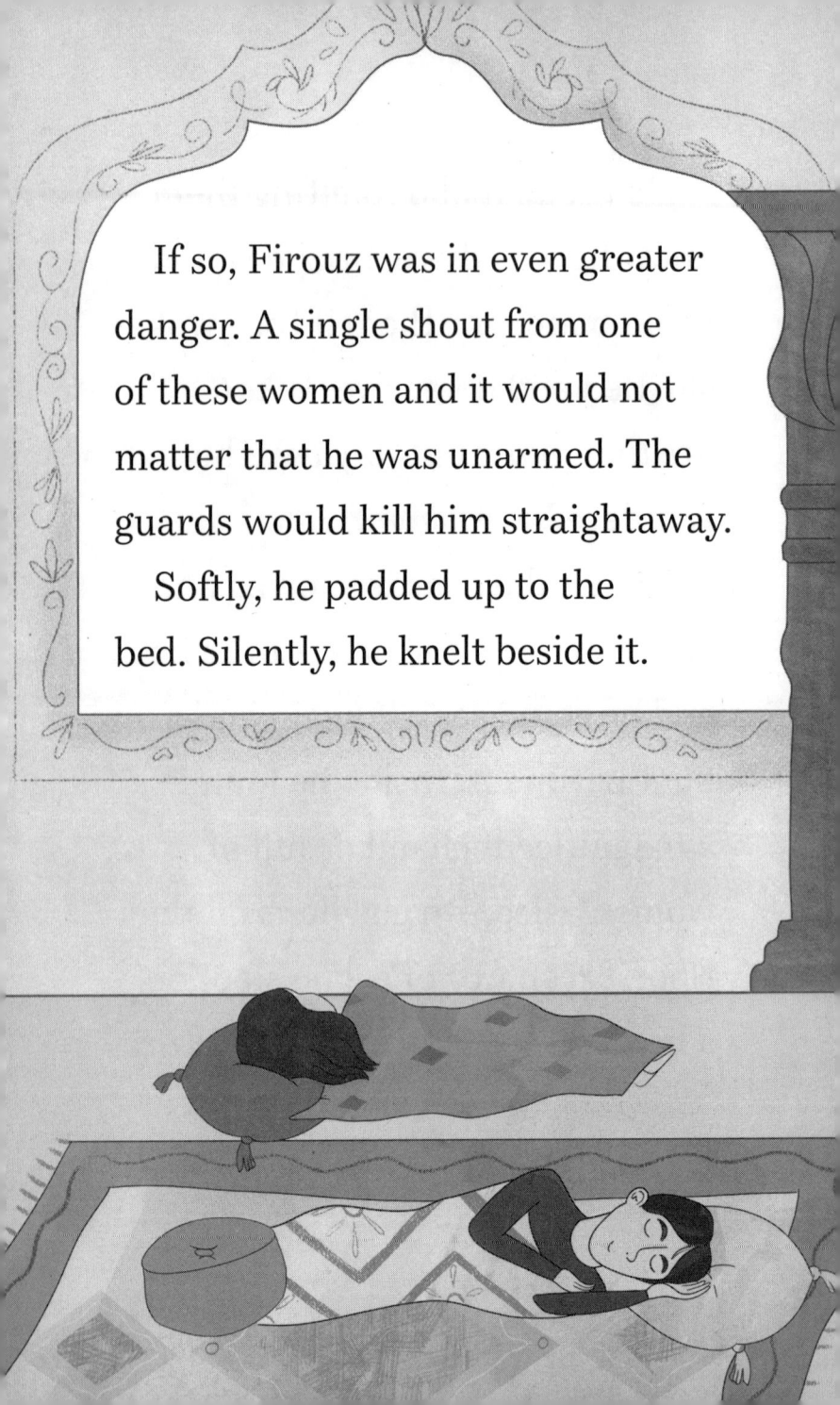

If so, Firouz was in even greater danger. A single shout from one of these women and it would not matter that he was unarmed. The guards would kill him straightaway.

Softly, he padded up to the bed. Silently, he knelt beside it.

Carefully, he reached out and touched the sleeping princess on the shoulder.

The princess woke and saw a strange man – but a kneeling one, so she did not immediately panic.

A new guard, perhaps? she thought.

Grateful for the princess's calmness and hoping that she understood Persian, Firouz took his chance to explain. 'Madam, you see before you a prince in distress. Just yesterday I was in my father's court, today by a strange adventure I am in yours. I ask for your protection.'

The princess listened kindly. 'Prince,' she assured him, 'you are welcome in Bengal. And though I am most curious to know how you have journeyed here, I will wait until you have rested to ask.'

She gave orders to her maids

to take Firouz to another room, which was just as lovely. While two of the women prepared a bed for him, the rest went to fetch food and drink.

The princess, after scolding her guards, found it impossible to fall back to sleep. The prince was very handsome, and she was very curious about him.

The moment her maids returned, the princess asked, 'What did you think of him?'

'Handsome!' replied one. 'Unlike the prince from India you rejected last month.'

'Kind,' replied another. 'Unlike the prince the month before – where was he from, again?'

All agreed that if the King of Bengal allowed it, their princess could not hope to find a better husband.

The princess tried not to look too pleased by these words. 'You are a bunch of chatterboxes,' she scolded them playfully. 'Go back to sleep.'

The next morning the princess dressed with great care. When her maids teased her about it, she replied, 'If the prince liked me as I was last night, think how much prettier he will find me when I have taken some care with my appearance.'

In her hair was placed the largest diamond she owned, and round

her neck and wrists her finest
necklace and bracelets. When she
was satisfied, she sent her maids
to see if the prince was ready
to see her.

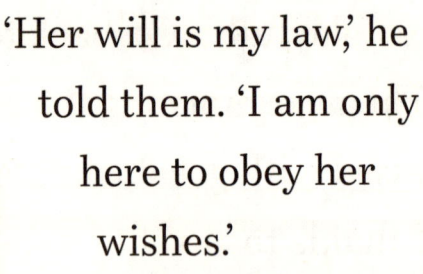

'Her will is my law,' he
told them. 'I am only
here to obey her
wishes.'

In a few
moments, the
princess appeared.
'You must forgive
my impatience,'
she told him. 'I
am dying to know

more about the strange adventure you mentioned. Now that you are rested, will you please tell me?'

So the prince told her about the Persian New Year celebrations, and his father who had a love for unusual inventions. He told her about the most unusual invention of all, the flying horse, and how it had brought him all the way to Bengal.

'I should have waited to hear the rest of the instructions before I turned the peg,' he admitted, 'but I did not think it would actually work! And the man was *so* rude. If I had another sister,

I would not let him marry her, however much our father wanted the horse.'

However handsome she found the prince, the princess was no fool. She listened to his story, and then she asked for proof that it was more than just that – a *story*.

The prince took her to the ebony horse, which was black and beautiful, just as he had described it. More importantly, it was large and heavy, and the courtyard was walled on all sides, with a single locked gate. How had it got inside if not by magic?

The princess toyed with the flowers wilting around the horse's neck. Flowers that did not grow locally.

'I believe you,' she said.

The prince was surprised.

'You do? I thought you would want me to fly it somewhere to show you.'

'I would rather you stay right here,' she told him, smiling shyly. 'I want to get to know you better.'

Firouz felt the same way. So even though he knew his father would be sleepless with worry about him, he stayed. And since Ameera's father would not approve of her staying with an unknown man, they kept it a secret.

As he and the princess got to know each other better, they grew to like each other even more. In time, Firouz revealed his fears that he would not be a good king after his father. Meanwhile the princess, whose name was Ameera, talked of her mother who had died when she was young. She also shared how all of her half-sisters had married before her, despite being younger.

'My father used to bring me a new suitor every month, but now I think he has quite given up,' she said. 'Perhaps I am too picky.'

'As you should be,' replied the prince. 'You deserve the very best of men.'

suitor
Someone who wants to marry someone specific.

'I agree,' Ameera said, looking straight at him.

Firouz blushed and looked away, into the lantern-lit palace that he now knew so well. It had been almost a month since his arrival.

The princess, having bribed her guards to look the other way, had shown Firouz every inch of her home.

'I would like to show you where I live,' he told her suddenly.

'I would like to see it. I have never been anywhere but here.'

'My home is very far away.'

'It is a good thing you have a flying horse, then.'

The prince laughed. 'I love–' He stopped. He had meant to say 'I love your sense of humour,'

bribe
To give someone something in return for them doing what you want them to do. Often secretive or dishonest.

but found himself wanting to say something else.

'*You*,' he concluded. He took the princess's hands in his. 'I love you, Ameera.'

She squeezed his hands. 'Then you really had better show me where you live.'

'Why is that?'

'So that I can ask your father's permission to marry you.'

The prince laughed again. '*You* are going to ask for *my* hand in marriage?'

'Well why not?' she replied. 'So many men have asked for mine that I would like to try the other way around for a change.'

Still laughing, the prince kissed her. It was at that moment that a voice boomed behind them. 'Unhand my daughter!'

Chapter 3

The King of Bengal saw his eldest daughter in the arms of a stranger, and then he saw red.

'Guards!' he roared. 'Seize him!'

The king's guards sprang from behind him. They were a different breed to the ones who protected the princess. Leaner, meaner – and under no bribe to let the princess do whatever she liked while keeping her secrets. Their swords were at the prince's throat before he could draw breath.

'Father, no!' cried Ameera.

'Who is this scoundrel?'

'He is no scoundrel at all – this is the Prince of Persia!'

The king frowned. 'What kind of prince sees a princess without her father's permission?'

'One who loves her,' replied Firouz.

'And I love him,' added Ameera.

The king paled unexpectedly. 'No,' was all he could say.

'No?' echoed Ameera. 'I thought you would be happy! I have finally met a man I wish to marry.'

'Happy to lose my favourite daughter?' replied the king. 'I think not.'

Suddenly it all made sense to Ameera – why every one of her

suitors had been so unsuitable, so easy to say no too. They had always been either too boring or too stupid or too ugly or too selfish – and sometimes all four.

'You never wanted me to accept their proposals …' she murmured.

'You are all I have left of your mother,' said the king. 'And they were not worthy of you. No man is – including this one. Take him away.'

There was a scuffle as the guards tried to drag Firouz away. Firouz struggled.

'Let me prove my worthiness!' he cried.

'How?' asked the king.

'I would suggest that we duel each other, but the princess loves you so much that I could never harm you. Choose your best guard and I will fight him instead. If I win, you agree to give your permission for us to marry.'

'You will defeat a single guard in return for my beloved daughter's hand? I think not.'

'Two guards, then.'

---

duel
A fight between two people using deadly weapons.

'It would not matter if you defeated *all* of them. It still will not prove you worthy of her.'

'And if I defeat your entire army?'

The king paused. The prince was not only handsome but well-built. It was possible that he could defeat the king's personal and household guards, but his army of thousands? Never. He would be killed and Ameera would stay home where she belonged, loving no man more than she loved her father.

'Very well,' said the king. 'Tomorrow morning you will meet my army in battle. If you win,' (and here he struggled not to laugh) 'you will marry my daughter, Princess Ameera.'

Since Firouz was a prince, he was shown to a comfortable room and not a prison cell. But it was as far from the princess as possible so he could not explain his plan to her, and she was unaware that he had one at all. Come dawn she was still pleading with her father to stand down his army.

'One man against thousands is not a fair fight!' she insisted.

'It was his suggestion,' said the king. 'You cannot blame me for it. Clearly he is one of your more stupid suitors.'

And, indeed, the prince did look foolish when he stood on the field of battle all alone opposite an army on horseback. He shouted over to where the king and his daughter watched from the side-line.

'At least let me have a horse!'

Feeling generous, the king waved a hand at a servant. 'Fetch him a horse from my stable.'

Too far away to hear but guessing what was being said, the prince called out again. 'I prefer to ride my own. He is in the princess's courtyard.'

The king nodded to the attendant and everyone waited for the prince's horse to be brought – not that it would make a difference to his fate. It took a very long time, and while the king grew very impatient, the princess began to understand what the prince was planning. She smiled across the field at him, and he at her. The king scowled.

At long last the ebony horse was dragged into view by no fewer than six men. Its hooves carved deep trenches in the mud and the sun bounced off its glossy back. It looked far less real in the light of day than it had that first night at the Persian court.

A murmur ran through the army. Then a ripple as shoulders began to bounce and heads to bob. They were laughing.

'I was wrong,' the king gasped, wiping tears from his eyes. 'This one is mad, not stupid!'

Unfazed, Firouz mounted the wooden horse, which only made the men laugh louder. Eventually the king called for silence. At his next order, the battle began. The front row of his army charged at the prince with a terrifying battle cry. Before they could reach him, however, Firouz turned the peg

in the horse's neck and flew right
over their heads. He landed neatly
behind them, while they clattered
and skidded to a halt.

The King of Bengal gasped. 'What is this magic?'

'It seems you were right about one thing, father,' said a smiling Ameera: 'the prince is not stupid.'

When the second row of men charged towards Firouz, he flew over their heads too. Then the third, and the fourth, until he had hopped and skipped his way to the back of the entire army. And as each row wheeled around to face him again, they tangled with each other. It looked more like they were fighting themselves!

'Ha!' the king laughed. 'Hahaha! Clever indeed!'

Unlike the soldier's horses, the magic horse never tired. It flew over their heads too high for them to reach with their swords, though they stabbed and jabbed at the air all the same. Like grass angling towards sunlight, their blades merely changed directions as the horse circled round and round. 'Enough!' the king wheezed,

clutching his sides. He had been laughing for almost as long as his soldiers had been falling over themselves. They lowered their weapons.

The king turned to his daughter. 'When you said this was not a fair fight, I assumed you were talking about your betrothed, not my men.'

Princess Ameera gasped. 'My betrothed? Then you give us permission to marry?'

While the king nodded and the princess threw her arms around his neck, Firouz landed nearby.

'Truly that it is a wonderful invention,' the king remarked, admiring the magic horse.

'Thank you, Your Majesty. It was a gift to my father.'

'That reminds me!' Ameera said. 'Since you are feeling generous, father. May we have permission to fly to Prince Firouz's court to see the King of Persia about our marriage?'

The King of Bengal liked the idea of his daughter riding such a magnificent invention, although he was a little too fearful to ride it himself. And he liked even more the knowledge that he was not the last to know of her romance with Prince Firouz, after all – the King of Persia was.

'Very well,' he agreed.

Chapter 4

Firouz was nervous about flying with a passenger – especially one as precious as the princess.

'Make sure you hold on to me,' he told Ameera more than once. 'It moves fast.'

'Good!' said Ameera, eager for an adventure. But she put her arms around his waist all the same.

Much more practised now at riding the magic horse, Firouz

pictured where he wanted to go exactly. It was not his father's palace, nor the great square where the New Year celebration had been held; it was a royal hunting lodge on the outskirts of town. Only when he could see it perfectly in his mind's eye did he turn the peg in the horse's neck. Immediately, Ameera's arms tightened around his waist as they leapt into the air. They looped once around the kingdom so that she could wave – carefully – at her people, and then they were off to Persia.

The horse travelled faster than ever. It would have travelled faster still if the prince had not spent so much time showing off, or the princess had not dared him to do this trick or that. They hurdled mountains, jumped off waterfalls and arrived at their destination breathless.

'What are we doing here?' Ameera asked, having expected to arrive at a palace.

The prince showed her to a beautiful set of rooms as he explained.

'First I must let my father know that I am alive. Then I will tell him that I am the happiest man – and why.' With this, the prince kissed Ameera's hands, mounted the magic horse and flew away to the palace. He would see to it that when he took Ameera with him, there would be a welcoming ceremony worthy of a princess.

As he flew, the people waved, overjoyed to see their prince after weeks spent believing that he was dead. But their relief was nothing compared to his father's. Firouz found the king surrounded by his advisors all dressed in black.

'Firouz!' cried the king.

'Your Highness!' cried the advisors.

After much joy and hugging, the king demanded to know all that had happened to the prince during his absence. Firouz told him in a rush, aware that Ameera was waiting for him.

'Father,' he said at the end, 'I have the King of Bengal's permission to marry his daughter and now I ask yours. Will you give it?'

'Gladly!' cried the king. 'You will be married today! It is the least I can do to repay the princess for giving you shelter all this

> **executed**
> *Historically, when someone was killed as punishment by law.*

time. The man who brought the magic horse is set to be executed tomorrow morning. We had given up hope of your return.'

'Set him free,' said the prince. He had long since forgotten his dislike of the man – or indeed his name, which was Sathvik. 'I owe him my thanks for causing me to meet the princess in the first place.'

So the king gave orders for Sathvik to be released from prison, and everyone changed out of their mourning clothes as

mourning
The feeling and expression of great sadness that follows a death or loss.

a concert of drums, trumpets and cymbals played in celebration of the crown prince's safe return.

Sathvik was brought before the king, who had not forgotten his anger as easily as the prince had forgotten his dislike.

'My son is safe,' he announced sternly; 'now so are you. You may take your life and your horse and begone forever.'

Just like that – after a month rotting in prison and still without the wife he had come for – Sathvik found himself dismissed. He left the palace angrily but quickly, before the king could change his mind. A servant took him to the magic horse, where Sathvik asked exactly what had happened to Prince Firouz while he was away. When he heard the story, and how a princess of Bengal was now waiting at the royal hunting lodge to marry Prince Firouz, he had an idea.

Sathvik flew to the lodge and was met by Princess Ameera. She had been watching anxiously from the window for Firouz's return. She was disappointed to find a stranger on the back of the magic horse instead of her prince.

'His Highness Prince Firouz asked me to fetch you to the palace,' Sathvik lied. 'He and the king are too busy with your wedding preparations to come themselves.'

In fact, at that very moment Firouz was riding a flesh-and-blood horse back to the lodge, having heard from his father that he planned to return the ebony one to Sathvik. Unaware of this, and too excited to ask questions, Ameera mounted the magic horse behind Sathvik and away they flew.

As extra revenge for his

imprisonment, Sathvik made sure to fly over the galloping prince's head as he stole away with his bride. Sathvik enjoyed the look of shock on Firouz's face, but when the princess saw it, she cried out in confusion.

'There is Firouz! What is happening? Take me down to him at once!'

Sathvik only made the magic horse fly higher. Soon they could not see the prince nor he them, and the princess's cries were snatched away by the wind.

'That wretch!' the king roared when Firouz had returned to the palace to report what had happened. 'He could be anywhere thanks to that monstrous horse of his!'

For his part, Firouz had moved past shock, through guilt and anger, and into quiet resolve.

'I *will* get Ameera back,' he vowed fiercely; 'magic horse or no magic horse.'

> **resolve**
> *The determination to get something done.*

Chapter 5

Without telling the king what he was doing, Firouz swapped his fine robes for the plain, rough clothes of a commoner. Knowing that the king might try to stop him, he did not share his plan. He did not even say goodbye, but left a note before he snuck out of the palace that night. The note said:

Forgive me, Father, for leaving again so soon. I will return with my bride or not at all.

Meanwhile, Sathvik had flown the magic horse to the kingdom of Kashmir and landed in woodland near the capital. The magic horse's hooves had not yet touched the ground when Ameera threw herself from its back and made to escape.

'Let go!' she yelled when Sathvik caught up with her, moving more slowly in his weakened state. 'Let go!' she repeated. 'Help! Help!'

Her screams alerted a nearby troop of horsemen. Following the sound, they found a well-dressed woman beating her fists furiously at a man who looked both ragged and half-starved.

'What is going on here?' the leader demanded to know – but he used a language that Ameera and Sathvik did not understand.

'She is my wife,' Sathvik said, hoping that at least one of the horsemen might understand Persian.

Ameera slapped him. 'I am not!'

'Ignore her, she is unwell.'

Wrenching herself free, the princess told the leader of the horsemen, 'If I am unwell, it is because I have been stolen from my prince on the very day of our wedding! Look! There is the magic horse he used to spirit me away!'

The horseman, who was none other than the Sultan of Kashmir, did in fact understand Persian.

sultan
A type of ruler or king in Islamic countries.

But he was convinced more by Ameera's beauty than her words that she was telling the truth (although not about the magic horse, of course). In his own language he said, 'Kill him.'

Immediately Sathvik was dragged behind a tree and beheaded.

The other riders inspected the wooden horse. They clearly had no idea how it could have got there, but its beauty was clear. The sultan's nod said that he wanted it for himself. While his men struggled to move the magic horse and take it with them, Ameera was pulled up in front of the sultan's saddle and carried away to his palace. There she was given the finest set of rooms to rest in and a selection of maids to wait on her. None of them spoke Persian, because the sultan did not want them to be able to speak to her.

'I want you to make her as comfortable as possible,' he told the maids.

Outside her apartment he placed his most faithful guards.

'No one is to go in or come out,' he told them.

The princess rested peacefully, trusting in the goodness of a sultan who had believed her so easily and treated her so kindly. Soon she would be back in the arms of Firouz, she told herself as she fell into a deep sleep.

She learnt better when the next morning she awoke to the sound of drums, trumpets and cymbals. For a moment she thought she was back in Persia as these were the same instruments that had sounded to celebrate Prince Firouz's return. Then she took in her strange surroundings and remembered her kidnapping.

Rubbing sleep from her eyes, Ameera went out onto the balcony. The sound of joyful music hit her like a wall.

'Have I interrupted a celebration?' she wondered out loud.

Thinking that she was alone, she had returned to using the language of her homeland, Bengal. It just so happened that although none of the maids spoke Persian, one of them spoke Bengali.

'It is more that you have ... *brought* a celebration,' said that same maid carefully.

'Oh!' Ameera startled, noticing the maid for the first time on the balcony with her. 'You can understand me!'

The maid shushed her with a finger to her lips. It was very rude thing for a servant to do to a princess, but Ameera lowered her voice all the same.

'What is it?'

The maid, whose name was Aditi, cast her eyes behind her at the other maids now entering with breakfast. She spoke again quietly so that they would not overhear. 'We are not supposed to talk to you.'

'Why ever not? And what do you mean that I have "brought" this celebration?'

'The music is in honour of our sultan's wedding.'

'What does that have to do with me?' Understanding dawned as soon as Ameera had asked the question. 'I must speak with the sultan at once!'

Again, Aditi shushed her nervously. 'You cannot tell him

that I told you. He will be furious – you were not to know until it was too late.'

'But I cannot marry him! I am engaged to another. I am sure if you help me to explain–'

'He understood you yesterday,' Aditi interrupted her. 'He does not care. He will wed you anyway, as soon as possible.'

The scale of the problem hit Ameera all at once. She was in a strange land whose strange ruler had no intention of letting her leave it. She fell dizzily against the wall.

'Your Highness!' a chorus of maids cried out – although Ameera did not understand what they said. While Ameera pulled herself back upright and stumbled indoors, they trailed behind her.

One held out a drink, another a cool, wet cloth and yet another tried to make her lie down.

'I am not sick!' Ameera insisted, slapping away a bottle of something she took to be medicine.

Ameera threw open the door to her rooms and found a row of guards standing outside them. There would be no escaping that way. She slammed the door shut again and ran back to the balcony. She already knew it was too high to risk jumping from but she leant so far over the edge to make sure that the maids pulled her back in a panic. Ameera pushed them away and ran to see if there were any other doors. There were not.

'What to do, what to do, what to do …' she repeated over and over, pacing back and forth and fisting her hair. Somewhere in this very palace was a flying horse that only she knew how to operate and she could not get to it!

This knowledge made her growl in frustration. From the corner of her eye, she saw the maids exchange worried glances. She stopped pacing. 'I have changed my mind – I *am* sick after all!'

With that, she set about destroying everything in sight. She tipped over tables covered with delicious treats. She smashed vases on the floor and dashed lanterns against the walls. She kicked her foot clean through an exquisite screen of cut woodwork. Then she set to shredding the silks on the bed and tearing the feathers from each couch pillow. All the while she wailed so loudly that the guards who were outside dared to come in. Like the maids, they shared worried glances.

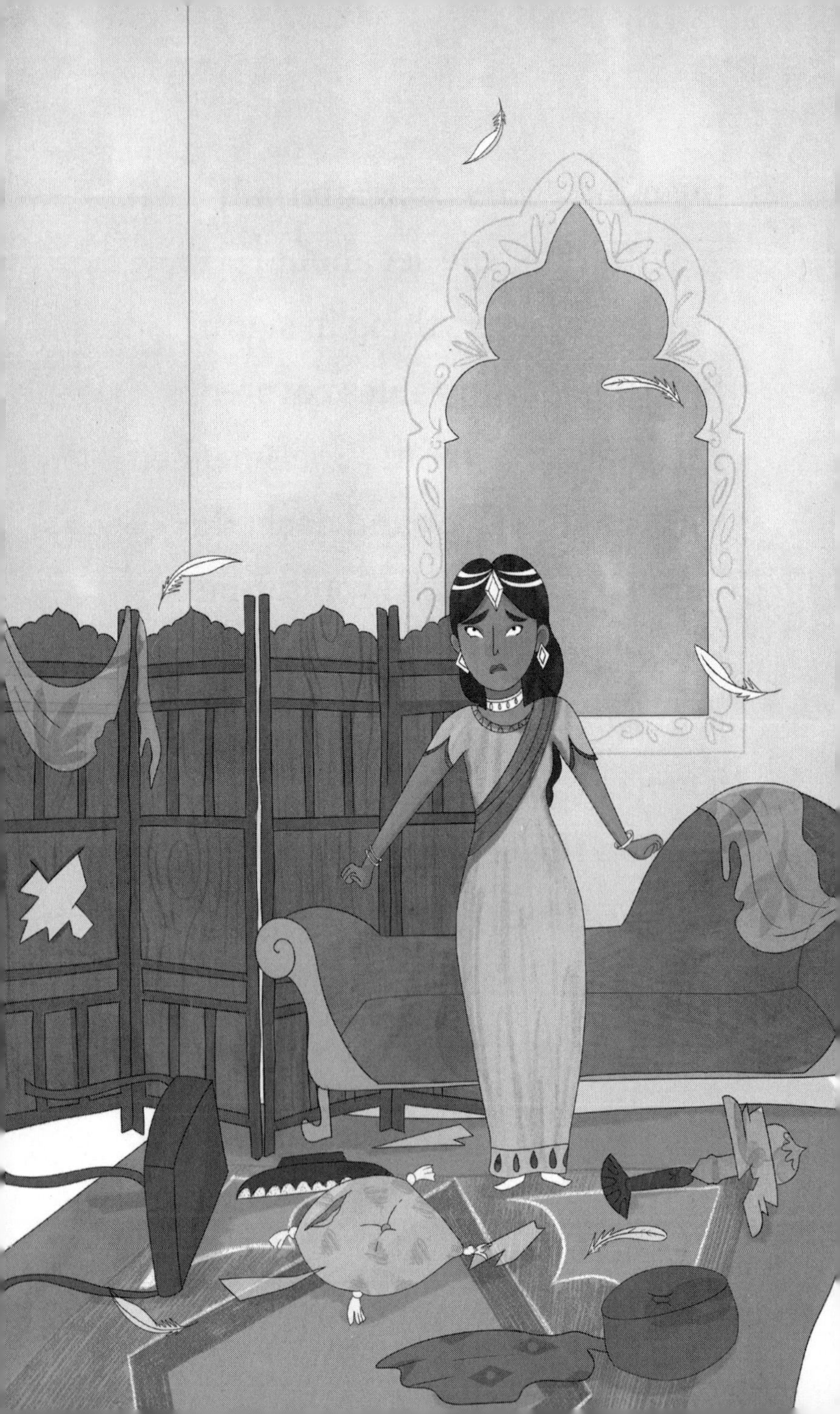

Clearly there was something wrong with their sultan's bride.

When the sultan came to visit, he found that he could not understand what Ameera was saying anymore. Surely *no one* could understand such ranting and raving. There would be no wedding that day, he realised sadly.

The only person who seemed able to calm the princess was the maid called Aditi. The rest of them were sent away.

'What was all that about?' Aditi asked when they were alone.

Ameera smoothed her wild hair

back from her face. 'Surely your sultan will not wish to marry me now.'

'You underestimate your beauty and his foolishness. Even now he is sending for people to cure you. How long can you keep up this act?'

'As long as I must,' answered Ameera. 'Until the sultan gives up and sets me free or Firouz finds me.'

'I will help you in any way I can,' Aditi promised.

Chapter 6

It soon became clear that the sultan would not give up easily. One by one, the doctors inspected the princess's condition. It was very difficult, as she would not let anyone but Aditi near her. When asked, Aditi told the doctors that the princess's pulse was very slow, but that her heartbeat raced. And her skin! Why her skin was ice cold one minute and burning with fever the next. Faced with these confusing lies, the court doctors ruled that there was no cure for the princess's illness.

As the days and weeks passed, rumours of the princess's illness spread far and wide, until they reached the ears of Prince Firouz. Sad and weary, he told himself not to get his hopes up. As the story travelled from person to person, the princess's name had changed from Ameera to Aamaal to Aarti to Maalai. By the time Firouz heard it, there was no name at all, only 'the unknown princess' whom the Sultan of Kashmir had rescued single-handed from a giant bear.

Nevertheless, Firouz set his course for the capital of Kashmir. When he arrived, he wanted nothing more than to go straight to the palace. But he made himself go to an inn first. There he listened to what the gossips had to say.

'If she could be cured, she would have been,' one man was

arguing. 'She has been seen by all our doctors and our neighbours' doctors now.'

'She must be very beautiful,' another man observed, 'for the sultan to go to all this trouble.'

'She must be very ungrateful!' growled the first. 'I hear she will not let him near her, despite his kindness – him or anyone else.'

'I heard she does not even speak our language,' a woman butted in.

Standing near them, Firouz cleared his throat. 'What was the princess's name again?' he asked in his best Kashmiri.

'Amal,' answered the first man, at the same time as the second said, 'Amara.'

The woman shook her head and corrected them. 'Her name is Ameera.'

Firouz could have wept with relief. It *was* her!

He cleared his throat again,

although this time it was to hide his excitement. 'Are they still allowing doctors to see her?'

'Yes,' sighed the first man, making it clear that he thought this was a waste of time. 'Why do you ask?'

Firouz told them that he was a doctor. He said he had been on the way to the palace to see the princess when he was attacked by bandits on the road.

'I would have been here much sooner otherwise,' he concluded. 'And yet I can hardly continue on to the palace like this.' He gestured to his dusty, travel-worn clothes.

The second man lit up. 'I know just the thing!'

So it was that Firouz was able to buy the robes of a doctor and disguise himself as one. After that there was nothing that could have kept him from going immediately to the palace and asking for an audience with the sultan.

The sultan was a tall, broad-shouldered man at least ten years older than Firouz. His first question was, 'You look too young to be a doctor as skilled as you claim to be.'

Firouz was thankful for the short beard that had covered his face since beginning his journey. He would look even younger without it.

'Your Majesty,' he assured the sultan, 'if you allow me to see the princess, I believe any doubts you have about my skills will be laid to rest.'

'You believe you can cure her?'

'I know it, Sire.'

The sultan was not convinced, but he led the way to the princess's rooms. 'It will be miracle enough if you can even get near her.'

They arrived at the princess's door, where the sultan knocked softly. His face was tense as they waited for a young maid to answer.

'How is she?' the sultan demanded.

'The same, Your Majesty. But she sleeps.'

With a sigh, the sultan made to go inside. Firouz stopped him.

'Forgive me, Sire, but it would be best if I could see the princess alone. We need her to be as calm as possible.'

The sultan agreed and Firouz entered the princess's apartment with the maid. There was little left in the way of furniture or decoration. What there was lay in shards, splinters and rags. They passed a balcony that had been blocked off by a metal gate and came to a bed in whose shredded sheets slept Ameera.

The maid, Aditi, opened her mouth to advise Firouz that he should not go any closer but he held a finger to his lips to quiet her. Already smiling to himself, he crept towards Ameera's sleeping form as he had on the night they met. He knelt beside her bed and gently touched her shoulder as he once had before.

The princess woke and saw a familiar man – the man she loved most in all the world.

'Firouz?' she breathed. 'Is it really you?'

In answer, the prince kissed her. Aditi looked away with a blush, quickly realising that this must be the Persian prince Ameera had spoken of.

'Have I cured you then?' Firouz laughed as he pulled away. 'All it took was a kiss?'

Ameera rolled her eyes. 'I had

to pretend to be sick or I would be married to the sultan right now.'

'He means to marry you without your consent?'

'He means to marry me without even asking!'

The princess told him everything that had happened to her since Sathvik stole her away.

'Where is the magic horse now?' Firouz asked.

'I do not know. Neither does Aditi.' Ameera nodded towards the maid. 'But now that you are here,' she added, 'I have an idea.'

> **consent**
> *To give consent is to give someone permission for *them* to do something. To have someone's consent is to have their permission for *you* to do something.*

Chapter 7

The princess was positive that the magic horse would be somewhere in the palace. She had seen the look on the sultan's face when he found it in the woods. And though she did not think he had believed her when she said that it was magic, there was no way he would have left it behind.

After Firouz left to inform the sultan that the princess was doing much better, Ameera combed her hair for the first time in days, and dressed with great care. When the Sultan returned with Firouz, she welcomed him.

The sultan was delighted by her improvement.

'You have not exaggerated your skills at all!' he told Firouz. 'You have done what no other doctor could.'

Firouz bowed modestly. 'Thank you for your compliments, Your Majesty. But my work is not yet done.'

'How long until she is fully recovered?'

'That will depend on how quickly I can find the source of her illness, Your Majesty. Am I right in thinking that your bride is from Bengal?'

'You are.'

Firouz looked thoughtful. 'May I ask how she came to be here?'

'She told me a story about a man kidnapping her on a magic horse. But it was nonsense.'

'Was the part about the kidnapper nonsense?'

'No,' the sultan admitted. 'That part was true. I had the villain executed on the spot.'

'And was there a horse?'

'Not a real one,' said the sultan. 'Only one made of ebony.'

'It may be that some form of dark magic from the horse has

attached itself to the princess and caused her sickness. Only by removing it can I cure her completely. Do you know where the horse is now?'

'It is in my treasury – but I tell you it does not even move, let alone fly.'

'Nevertheless, Sire, for the sake of the princess's recovery, I must ask you to let me see it. If the horse and the princess could be brought together outside in the open air, I will burn herbs to rid the magic from both of them.'

> **treasury**
> *A place where money and other valuable things are kept.*

'Very well,' agreed the sultan.

As with everything to do with the princess, word spread. The people soon learnt that a doctor was halfway to curing her, and that the final half would take place outside. Add to that the rumour that a magic horse was somehow involved and there was no way to avoid an audience.

While the public surrounded the palace square, the sultan seated himself on a raised platform with the nobles of his court. They had the best view as Princess Ameera appeared. She walked straight up to the wooden horse in the centre of the square and mounted it with help from the doctor.

Firouz lit fires at each corner of where the horse was standing, and onto the burning coals he cast a handful of perfumed herbs. As the herbs caught fire and crackled and began to smoke, Firouz walked three times around the horse, muttering something none of the onlookers could hear. Before he had completed his third circle, heavy smoke began to billow from the fires. It was so thick that soon the onlookers could not see him or the princess.

In a flash, Firouz mounted the magic horse behind Ameera

and put his arms around her waist. With the reins in one hand, Ameera turned the peg in the horse's neck with the other.

They rose into the air with the billowing smoke, above the crowd, above the court – above the sultan himself, who gaped up at them.

Ameera shouted down, 'Consider this my answer to the question you never bothered asking!'

The couple flew back to Persia and were married as soon as the King of Bengal could join them. Ameera even arranged for Aditi to come and work at the palace as the first of her ladies and her most trusted friend.

A month after the wedding, husband and wife headed quietly to the king's gallery of inventions.

They passed the golden peacock that told the hours and the brass trumpet that alerted you to danger. They went straight to the ebony horse.

'Where shall be go next?' Firouz asked.

Ameera reached for the red velvet saddle.

'Everywhere,' she answered.